The Jigsaw Puzzle

Ros Gemmell

Also by Ros Gemmell

Summer of the Eagles

For Adults as Romy Gemmell

Dangerous Deceit
Mischief at Mulberry Manor
The Aphrodite Touch

Coming Soon

Midwinter Masquerade

The Jigsaw Puzzle

Ros Gemmell

www.rosemarygemmell.com

Published in 2013 by FeedARead.com Publishing –
Arts Council funded

Cover Artist C.K. Volnek

First published as an ebook 2013 by MuseItUp
Publishing, Canada

A CIP catalogue record for this title is available from the British Library.

For Lauren, Keira and Connor. Enjoy the magic of childhood.

Acknowledgements

Grateful thanks to publisher Lea Shizas and excellent content editor Susan Davis for bringing the original ebook to publication. Huge thanks to wonderful cover artist C.K. Volnek.

With much gratitude to my own dearly departed parents who provided me with a safe, fun and magical childhood.

The Jigsaw Puzzle

Chapter One

Daniel sensed something strange about the jigsaw as soon as Amy insisted they put it together. It started with that weird dream before he got there... *He was walking down a long path in a colourful garden, leading to a sundial where the shadow cast by the sun showed it was just after midday. Then, the picture changed. He seemed to be running from room to room inside an old house, with a girl beside him. His asthma caused him to take great gasps as it got harder to breathe. They were looking for a way out...*

This was the first weird dream he ever remembered so clearly. He could even picture the details and feel the panic. But why was he so out of breath and frightened in a strange old house?

Now, here he was staying with his Aunt Jill and Cousin Amy for the rest of the Christmas holidays because his mum and dad had gone off to America without him. And he couldn't believe it when the girl in his dream turned out to be his cousin! He'd never been to their cottage before. That should have warned him this was going to be no ordinary visit.

He told himself not to be silly. At school, Mrs Preston kept telling him he had too much imagination. And he loved reading creepy stories, or adventures, imagining himself the hero, though with his wheezy chest and skinny body he hardly looked anything like an Indiana Jones.

Daniel hadn't shown how much he cared as he waved goodbye to his mum and dad. Imagine going all the way to America without him because Dad might be going to work there. Mum didn't look too happy about leaving Daniel, and he didn't want her to worry. Besides, he had no intention of showing Amy how much he'd miss his parents. It was only for a couple of weeks. Anyway, he was fed up with them arguing all the time and he hoped they'd sort things out, but he didn't want to have to move to America.

After he watched his parents climb inside their new flashy silver car and drive away down the country road until they were out of sight, Daniel turned around and nearly bumped into Amy. She'd obviously been watching him.

"Mum says we can have some juice and biscuits, so I've poured the orange squash out for you," Amy said. "Let's go and have it now."

Daniel shrugged and followed her. He didn't know his cousin very well. She seemed okay so far, not too girly, though a bit bossy. Amy wore scruffy jeans and a sweatshirt. Her short, fair hair stuck out in all directions as though she hadn't brushed it for a week, a bit different from his combed brown hair. But he guessed that might change while living here.

Aunt Jill was in the kitchen. "You make yourself at home, Daniel," she said. "Amy will show you everything and I'll see you both at tea time." She absent-mindedly hugged him. "I'm away upstairs to do some more painting."

Daniel smelled a mixture of paint and white spirit from her hands before she went off to her work room. He'd heard artists were sometimes a bit distracted from real life when working. He didn't mind being left with Amy—better than being fussed over. He hoped his aunt would show him some of her paintings before he returned home.

As he and Amy sat on the living room floor with their juice and biscuits, Daniel noticed a sudden movement on his left. Then a small ginger cat rubbed its head against his leg. He didn't know they had cats.

"Hope you like cats," Amy said as she held out her hand. "Here, Spicy, leave Daniel alone. We've got a black cat as well called Inky, but he's a bit shy."

"Cool! I love all kinds of animals, but Mum won't let me have any pets in case it makes the asthma worse."

Daniel hoped he wasn't allergic to cat fur. His mum would have a fit if she saw them. Amy only shrugged and stroked Spicy's amber coat.

"What d'you want to do?" Amy jumped up and pushed Spicy aside. "It's still a bit wet to explore outside. Come on an' I'll show you round the house and we'll look for something to do."

He'd never met such a bossy boots, but Daniel didn't mind for today. He followed as she wandered from room to room. He wanted to see the rest of the house. It reminded him a little of the dream but not exactly, and he decided to forget all about it. Probably just a coincidence he now stood inside a cottage after dreaming about one.

"There're three bedrooms upstairs—one for me, one for Mum, and a spare one for you," Amy said. "The other room is Mum's studio where she paints, that's where she is just now. She doesn't like to be disturbed when she's there," Amy whispered.

"There's a bathroom at the end of the landing and an attic at the top of the house, but you need to pull down the ladder to get up to it. We can climb up there another day."

Daniel wanted to ask about her dad and then remembered she didn't have one. He'd once heard his mum and dad talking about Aunt Jill and how she wouldn't marry Amy's dad.

He reckoned no one would ever guess his aunt and mother were sisters. Aunt Jill seemed younger than his mum, tying her long, fair hair up in a scarf and she wore old jeans and a paint-spattered T-shirt. His mum always dressed smartly and got her light brown hair done at the hairdressers every month. She'd never be seen dead in anything so tatty.

"I know what we'll do." Amy suddenly ran into her room, startling him out of his thoughts. "I found an old jigsaw in the attic one day and I haven't tried it yet. Let's take it downstairs and we could start it now."

Hardly pausing to see if Daniel agreed, Amy led the way down to the living room as though expecting him to follow. So, he did. He didn't really care what they did today. Anything would do to stop him picturing his mother and father driving away without him.

He didn't even want to *think* about them flying across the Atlantic to America with the kinds of trouble these days, or accidents. *No, don't think of that.* At least Amy kept him amused in her bossy way, taking charge. He used to like jigsaws and hadn't done one for years. In fact, he loved any kind of puzzle, especially anything in code. It was a change from playing computer games, though his friend back at school, Paul, would never believe Daniel put together a jigsaw.

Once seated at the big table in the corner, they opened the jigsaw box, standing the picture lid against the fruit bowl so they could see it clearly. Hundreds of small pieces lay in the box. Daniel picked one up, surprised to find the pieces made of thin wood instead of cardboard. It appeared very old and cut a bit differently from more modern jigsaws.

Some of the curved edges had no cut-out bit to attach to another piece. He reckoned they probably shaped against another curve to join up. Other pieces looked more like the kind he knew with notches or spaces to connect to each other.

Daniel stared at the picture on the lid. "Huh, a house and garden. Why can't it be something interesting like wild cats or birds?"

Amy shrugged, not bothering to answer. She might be bossy, Daniel thought, but at least she didn't chatter all the time like the girls at school.

Then he stared at the picture more closely, noticing something strange about it. The house did look a bit familiar. But the old-fashioned crisscross windows had tiny panes of glass which he'd never seen before. A strange doorknocker shaped like an old face hung on the door, and the garden bloomed with lots of colourful flowers and plants. A stone sundial stood at the bottom of the garden, casting a shadow across its surface. Daniel's stomach flipped. The house in his dream!

He glanced at Amy, who kept picking up jigsaw pieces.

"Don't you think the house in the picture looks a bit like your house, Amy, only older?" he asked.

Amy studied the picture for a few minutes before replying, "I guess so. I thought it looked familiar when I found it in the attic. It's odd isn't it? And the jigsaw looks quite old."

Then she shrugged as usual and tipped all the jigsaw pieces onto the table in a pile. "Let's find the edges first and start with the garden."

Daniel did jigsaws that way, too, finding the edges and corners first. Just as well, since bossy Amy took charge of the order. But it didn't matter. He'd let her be as bossy as she wanted, for now. It was fun sitting at the big table while the rain poured down outside the window and drummed against the door.

Daniel pictured his mum and dad at the airport, maybe they'd even be on the plane by now. No, he wasn't going to think of them flying across the Atlantic Ocean. They'd come back safely and they'd all go home together again. And Dad might get a new job in Scotland and wouldn't be so angry all the time.

Right now, Daniel wanted to enjoy putting together this jigsaw with Amy. He stared at the picture of the cottage on the lid. Strange, it looked exactly like the house in the dream and like the one they sat in, except the jigsaw house appeared older, as if from a long time ago.

Only an old jigsaw, Daniel decided as he put the first pieces of the garden into place. Nothing strange in that, was there?

Chapter Two

The first part of the jigsaw turned out to be more difficult than they expected. Too many flowers grew close together and lots of them looked the same. Daniel and Amy searched for the bottom corners of the puzzle and each put the straight-edged pieces into a pile of their own.

By the afternoon, when the rain finally stopped, they'd completed one corner of the jigsaw. Then Aunt Jill called down to them.

"Amy, Daniel, can you run along to the village shop for some milk before it gets any darker? I'm going to make the meal shortly."

They put the lid on the box and examined what they'd done so far. The whole bottom right section of the jigsaw fitted together. It showed the corner of the garden with the sundial and lots of brightly coloured flowers. Not very exciting, Daniel thought.

As Amy collected some money from a purse in the kitchen, he asked, "So, do you go to the shop by yourself all the time?"

"Of course I do. I'm not a little kid. It's only the wee shop down at the bottom of the path by the woods and everybody knows me here in the village. Why? You're not goin' to tell me you don't go to the shops on your own?"

"Not that often." Daniel ignored her sarcasm. "Except to the shop near the school during lunch time. Mum does all the shopping at the big supermarket in town." He couldn't admit to Amy that his mum worried about him far too much. He hardly got to do anything on his own. It was so embarrassing at his age.

To reach the shop, they walked quickly through the overgrown trees and bushes in the wooded area until they reached the path. Frost already formed patterns on the leaves and stones scattered over the hard ground. Daniel lifted his jacket collar up around his ears. Amy had pulled a woolly hat over her head when they left the house.

More trees lay ahead, but the path to the shop veered right and led them down a short hill in the opposite direction from the woods. A few more metres and Daniel could see the shop on the main village street.

The old-fashioned small shop had a polished wooden counter, and tall jars of sweets stood on the shelf behind. The rest of the shop displayed the usual things like newspapers, a cold cabinet for milk, butter, and cheese, a shelf with boxes of fruit and vegetables, and shelves with all kinds of cans and jars.

Daniel had no idea where they'd find the nearest supermarket, but it probably didn't matter for some things. The shop seemed friendly and warm. Daniel guessed the people who lived in the village met each other here for a chat while they did their shopping, like in olden days.

"Hello, Amy." The tall shopkeeper had a friendly grin. "Who's your wee friend today?"

"This is my cousin, Daniel. He's staying with us for a while, Mr Ferguson."

"Well, ah hope ye have a great wee holiday, Daniel. Will ye both be stayin' up for Hogmanay then, to see in the New Year?"

"Yes, I think so," Amy replied.

Daniel glanced at Amy. Cool. He'd never been allowed to stay up that late before, until midnight. He didn't even know if his mum and dad bothered staying up to greet the New Year on their own. Some of his friends' parents had a party at their homes and invited all the neighbours to bring in the New Year with them, but his mum and dad didn't seem that neighbourly.

He'd probably seem a bit of a wimp if he said anything about never staying up that late before. Sometimes his mother treated him like a five-year-old rather than his twelve years. He knew it was maybe because he nearly died when born. Then the asthma gave them a few scares over the years. And he didn't have any brothers or sisters for his mum to think about. Maybe this holiday with his scruffy cousin and distracted aunt would turn out to be a good idea after all. Give him a chance to do different things.

"Any sweeties for you today, Amy?" Mr Ferguson asked.

"Could we have some sherbet lemons, please?"

Daniel nearly said "what?" out loud. His mum didn't allow him to eat hard sweets or any other kind between meals. Aunt Jill mustn't be as strict as his mum, which didn't surprise him. He wondered what Amy's teeth were like. Maybe she had lots of fillings.

Daniel watched as Mr Ferguson poured the hard yellow sweets into an old-fashioned weighing scale then popped them into a white paper bag.

"Bye, Amy, bye, Daniel. Enjoy your holiday, son," Mr Ferguson called as they left the shop.

As they walked back along the street, Amy held out the bag of sweets. "Here, have one, Daniel."

He took one while he had the chance. Since his mum wouldn't know about it he might as well enjoy it.

As they wandered toward the path, Daniel sucked the hard sherbet lemon, rolling it around his mouth so he could enjoy the sweet taste. Then suddenly the sour sherbet in the thin middle hit the back of his throat. He coughed, choking for a second.

"You okay?" Amy stared at him and then laughed. "Oh, it's the sherbet, isn't it? It's always a surprise when the sweet dissolves and the sharp taste bites through."

Still coughing, Daniel couldn't believe he'd never had a sherbet lemon before. He sometimes ate chocolate, but the only other crunchy sweets he'd eaten were from the boys at school. The sweet taste of the hard sticky lemon followed by the sudden burst of sharp fizz was cool, even if it did make him choke.

On the climb back up the short hill, Daniel breathed the coldness into his lungs, making it difficult to get enough air. He wheezed, his chest rattling a bit, and finally had to stop for a moment to find his inhaler. He often got into trouble for leaving it lying about somewhere. Relief washed over him when he found it in his jacket pocket.

"Is it still the sherbet making you gasp?" Amy asked. Then she noticed the inhaler. "Oh, I forgot, you said you've got asthma. Does the coldness make it worse?"

When he nodded, she said, "One of the girls at school has an inhaler with her all the time. I've seen her use it. She sort of sprays it into her mouth. Seems to make it better."

Huh, Amy seemed a right know-all about everything. Daniel opened the inhaler cover and breathed in a puff of the fine spray as Amy watched with interest.

"Does it help right away?" Amy asked as Daniel shoved the inhaler back in his pocket.

"Near enough. Sorry, we can start walking again. The very cold weather's the worst thing for it, and I sometimes get breathless after gym at school." He didn't tell her it sometimes happened when he got upset or worried, like when his mother and father had a long argument.

"Where do you go to school?" he asked Amy. He hadn't seen anything remotely resembling a school so far.

"I'm going to high school in the next town after summer. There's a bus for the villagers. I used to go to the wee local school on the other side of the village. There're more children than you think around here—lots of them live on farms or in remote cottages like ours. I've got one special friend, but he's at his gran's over the holidays."

Somehow, Daniel just knew her best friend would be a boy. He'd never known a more tomboyish girl. "I'm going to high school, too, near Glasgow," Daniel said. "Most of my friends are going as well, so it maybe won't be so strange."

"I can't wait," Amy confided. "I'm fed up with the village school. It'll be great to be in a bigger town and go to lots of different classes. I want to learn more about languages, so I can travel round the world one day."

They walked in silence for a while and soon reached the top of the path at the side of the woods. Darkness was beginning to fall and Daniel noticed a faint moon visible beyond the trees. He shivered. The woods looked a little creepy and only one weak street lamp lit the narrow path they used. He wouldn't like to walk here on his own in the dark. Frosty leaves crunched underfoot and he tried not to imagine that someone followed them.

Then, just around the corner, they reached the flat open area leading to the cottage, and he felt foolish having such silly ideas. Amy probably never gave the path a second thought. Daniel remembered a question he wanted to ask before they went inside.

"Amy, do you mind if I ask you something?"

She stopped walking. "Well…as long as it's not *too* serious."

It was serious to him, but he tried to lighten up a bit.

"Just wondered if you ever missed your dad?"

Amy thought for a moment. "I never really knew him, so I suppose it didn't matter all that much. Mum and I get on great and she lets me take care of myself a lot. Sometimes, when I see other dads at parents' nights and so on, I wonder what it would be like, but mostly I don't think about not having one. Why d'you want to know?"

Surprisingly, Daniel knew Amy might be the very person to talk to. She was so down to earth and practical that she'd tell him what she thought.

They slowly walked on again as Daniel told her about his mum and dad arguing and about America. "I don't want them to split up," he finished. "And I don't want to go to America!"

"Och, there're a few kids in my class whose parents no longer live together, but they seem okay about it. Maybe some people get on better when they live apart."

Daniel thought about what she said. Maybe it'd be better than his sleep being so disturbed by the arguing. He hated the tight feeling in his chest at their raised voices, so he wouldn't miss that. But he loved his dad and couldn't imagine not seeing him each day.

"Thanks," he said. He was glad when Amy only smiled and quickened their pace. He didn't want to bore her.

When they got back to the house, Amy went to help her mum in the kitchen. Daniel wandered out to the back garden, looking for the cats, although it was getting a bit dark to see clearly. Some light shone from the kitchen and he was curious to see if the garden looked anything like the one in the jigsaw picture, as he hadn't seen it properly since he came.

A paved path stretched down the middle of the garden and he followed it toward the big tree at the bottom. No sign of the cats. He was almost to the tree, when he suddenly stopped.

Something *did* seem strangely familiar. Then he saw it. He moved nearer to investigate and stared, surprised. A stone sundial. Just like the one in the jigsaw, and the one in his dream. He ran up the path and dashed in the back door, calling for Amy.

Chapter Three

"What's wrong with you?" Amy hurried out from the kitchen. "Seen a ghost?"

"Come and see, Amy, it's the strangest thing." He half pulled her down the garden path until he got near the tree again. "In there, look!"

"What am I supposed to be looking for?" She sounded grumpy and impatient, but she peered in amongst the plants. Then she stood up. "Daniel, look. A sundial!"

"That's what I'm trying to tell you. It's like the one in the jigsaw. Has it always been here?"

Amy screwed up her eyes to think. "No, I don't think so. At least, I've never noticed it before."

Puzzled, they discussed it as they walked back to the house. Daniel wondered if his aunt would know about the sundial. Then they both had the same thought.

"Let's do some more of the jigsaw after tea," Amy said.

Daniel wasn't so sure about it, but he couldn't wimp out already.

"So, what have you two been getting up to?" Aunt Jill asked as they ate their meal together at the kitchen table.

"Oh, just an old jigsaw I found in the attic," Amy answered. "The picture on it looks a bit like this house, isn't that funny?"

Jill looked up in interest. "That's probably the one my great grandmother painted a long time ago. It *is* this house, or at least it's the way it looked when she lived here, in Victorian times."

Daniel and Amy looked at each other but didn't say anything.

Aunt Jill continued, "She painted, too, and I think someone in the village used to make puzzles. He made her picture into the jigsaw. But I don't know if anyone's ever put it together. It must have been in that attic for donkey's years."

"I didn't know they made jigsaws in the olden days," Amy said.

"Neither did I at first, but I recently read about the first one being made back in the seventeen hundreds. It was a map to teach British children geography, would you believe."

"Hey, that's a great idea," Amy said. "Much less boring than listening to old Batters droning on."

Her mum sighed and shook her head. "Amy, I've told you not to call Mr Battersea that."

Amy giggled and grinned at Daniel.

Aunt Jill said, "I remember my grandmother telling me about *her* mother, my great grandmother. She was an unusual woman for her time. People used to say she had some kind of special power, but I'm sure that was all nonsense. She was just a bit different from other women and lived alone for a long time after her husband died, getting on with her paintings. The house has been done up over the years since then, of course, modernised and painted and such like."

Daniel listened so hard he didn't realise he'd stopped eating.

"Your chicken is going to get cold, Daniel, if you don't hurry up and eat it. Or Amy will scoff it for you." His aunt laughed as Amy scowled at her.

"Anyway, great grandmother *was* a very special woman. She used to say everything she painted had a little bit of her love in it. And I know she really loved this cottage and felt very protective of it." She paused to eat another forkful of dinner.

Daniel noticed that Amy listened as intently as he did, although she'd munched her way through all her dinner first.

Aunt Jill continued the story, "My gran told me the cottage must always stay in the family, that no one outside should ever own it. I thought it might be sold when Gran died because my parents didn't want it. But Gran left it to me and Amy. I guess she knew how much I loved it, too."

Daniel finished the chicken and potatoes and then asked the question that had been puzzling him, "Aunt Jill, does that mean your great grandmother was Amy's great, great grandmother?"

"Yes, that's right. But she was yours as well, Daniel."

He stared in surprise, then realised what she meant. "Because you and my mum have the same parents, of course! My Gran and Grandpa McGregor are also Amy's gran and grandpa."

His aunt laughed. "Absolutely right, so my great grandmother would be very happy to know that both her great, great grandchildren are here now. And even more pleased to know you're interested in art, too, Daniel. We've always been a family of artists through the years."

Daniel glanced at Amy again. What a lot to think about. He wondered about his great, great grandmother. Maybe she bewitched the jigsaw with her protective love. He nearly laughed out loud. Talk about too much imagination! They'd only found an old jigsaw, and Aunt Jill had told them it *was* a painting of this house. So no real mystery, was there?

But he had to ask, “Aunt Jill, do you have a sundial at the bottom of the garden?” He ignored Amy’s frown.

His aunt thought for a moment before she answered, “I know there used to be one a long time ago, but I thought Gran had got rid of it at some point. Would you believe I haven’t really looked at the garden that much since we moved here? It’s one of the jobs I keep meaning to attend to so I suppose it could still be there. I’m finishing the latest commission before I tackle the garden in spring.”

Daniel could believe it. Aunt Jill seemed completely engrossed in her illustrations at the moment. But he grinned at Amy. That was the answer then. The sundial had always been there, and Amy just hadn’t noticed it.

Then his aunt turned to him. “You must come and see my paintings one of the days while you’re here, Daniel, if you’re interested.”

“Cool, thanks!” She really was so friendly, and he loved that she didn’t make a fuss about anything. He saw Amy making strange faces at him and guessed he shouldn’t say anything more about the jigsaw for now.

They helped clear away the food and dishes. Then, when Aunt Jill went back upstairs, they did a bit more of the jigsaw. Trying to fill in the whole bottom section, they eventually fitted each piece of the flowers into the right place. The garden section was complete.

“Let’s have a quick look at the back garden before it’s time for bed,” Amy suggested. “We can put the kitchen lights on and there’s a light outside. Anyway, I’ve got a torch.”

“But won’t your mum think it strange if we go out at this time in the dark?” Daniel wasn’t sure he wanted to see any more tonight.

Amy laughed. “Mum won’t be down for ages yet, and we can say we’re letting the cats in. I’ll hold your hand if you’re scared of the dark.”

He wasn’t worried about the dark and Daniel grinned to show he didn’t take her seriously. Shrugging on their jackets, they set off down the garden path.

With the light from the house and torch, their eyes soon grew accustomed to the darkness. They reached the bottom of the garden near the sundial and peered around in the dark.

“There’re masses of flowers,” Daniel whispered. “I don’t remember seeing all these before dinner when I came down here.” How weird was that? And he began to feel a little bit nervous. “Where did they all come from? It’s supposed to be winter.”

Amy stared at him in the twilight and then shrugged. “Och, we’d better wait and look properly tomorrow when it’s light. We’re probably just imagining there’re more.”

Daniel was relieved to hurry back up to the house and close out the night. He didn’t like the bit about the great grandmother having special powers. Maybe it *was* nonsense like Aunt Jill said, or maybe not. Great grandmother had painted the jigsaw picture of the cottage she loved and wanted to protect, and now something strange seemed to be going on. There had to be, especially after the dreams he’d been having about the house.

He wasn’t sure he wanted to do another part of the puzzle, but Amy would laugh at him if he said anything. Maybe the dream he had before he came to her house was a warning. But a warning about what?

Chapter Four

Next morning, Daniel woke up and yawned. He'd been restless through the night, dreaming about the woods again, but not the house. It *looked* like the woods they'd walked past yesterday.

After breakfast, Amy grabbed hold of him. "Let's go and look at the garden again."

Daniel fetched his jacket and followed her outside. The black cat, Inky, shot out of the house with them and slinked away down the garden. They wandered slowly along the overgrown path.

"Look!" Amy pointed. "D'you not think there're far too many flowers for this time of year? Hey, isn't that like the yellow bush in the jigsaw picture?" She stopped near a huge flowering plant.

It reminded Daniel of the one that grew in his garden in the summer, a potent… something. But it was now winter and all those other flowers shouldn't be looking so *alive*.

"This is too wacky," Amy said, followed by a nervous sounding laugh. She moved over beside the sundial to see if it worked. Daniel thought it didn't look that old. It seemed quite clean with a definite shadow darkening one part of it.

"I don't think we should do any more of the jigsaw," Daniel suggested. "These flowers shouldn't be here at this time of year, but they're in the jigsaw picture. Who knows what might happen next."

"Och, I still think we're imagining it," Amy said. "Maybe we could do a little bit more, then we'll know for sure there's nothing wrong with it. What about a bit of the house? That's not likely to change."

Amy might laugh at him for even thinking such a ridiculous thing could happen, but Daniel wasn't so sure.

"I don't know, Amy. I've got a funny feeling about that jigsaw."

Maybe he should have told Amy about the strange dreams. She'd probably laugh at him again in that sarcastic way she had. He'd wait a while longer, see if anything else happened. As if it could!

They wandered back to the house and found Spicy, the ginger cat, sitting on the doorstep. Daniel bent down to stroke him and the cat suddenly stood up and arched his back, tail in the air.

"What's wrong with Spicy?" It gave him a fright. Surely he hadn't spooked the cat?

"That's funny, he doesn't usually behave like that," Amy said.

Then they heard the front door bell.

"Oh, he must have known someone was at the door," Daniel said with relief. He'd read that cats could often sense things before humans. Like dogs being able to hear high-pitched sounds people couldn't hear.

As they hurried inside the cottage, they heard voices at the front door and took a quick peek to see who was talking. A tall, thin man with a beard looked as though he was explaining something, and Aunt Jill didn't look or sound very happy.

Daniel and Amy caught a little of the conversation.

"You must be joking! What gives you the right to come here at this time of year with nonsense like this?" Aunt Jill spoke loudly.

Daniel had never heard her voice raised so much. They couldn't hear what the man was saying. Amy crept closer to the action without being seen and grinned at Daniel, finger to her lips to make sure he stayed quiet.

Then the door banged shut. They hurried back into the kitchen, sat at the table, and waited to see what had happened.

"You two are very quiet. Have you fallen out?"

They jumped as Aunt Jill appeared in the kitchen doorway. She looked a bit worried.

"Oh no, we're just a bit tired." Daniel rubbed his eyes to make it look like the truth.

"Well, have an early night tonight," his aunt said. "Tomorrow is Hogmanay and you can stay up late to welcome in the New Year."

"Great!" Daniel said. He'd never brought in the New Year before and often wished he had after some of his friends had talked about it. It was definitely going to be more fun staying with Aunt Jill and Amy than he'd hoped. He liked this part of Scotland, too, for the countryside was much better than the busy, noisy town where he lived. He'd even managed to stop missing his mum and dad, except when he thought about them too much. They were probably having a great time in America.

Then he remembered the jigsaw. What if something strange *was* going on? And the talk of Hogmanay had made them forget about the commotion at the door a few minutes ago. What was that all about?

"Who was that man?" Amy asked.

Daniel liked the way she just came right out and said things or asked questions.

Aunt Jill sat down on one of the kitchen chairs. "You'll never believe what that man came here for." She still sounded angry. "He said they're going to start building a new road through the village sometime in the New Year, and that the cottage and the woods are in the way. They want to pull down the cottage, would you believe? *And* destroy the woods. Can you believe that? Coming here between Christmas and New Year to tell me something like that! Said we'd be hearing more about it early in January."

Daniel stared at his aunt and Amy. It couldn't be true, surely.

"But they can't just knock down our house," Amy cried. "There must be something we can do, or a law against it. This is our home! It was left to us. *And* it's been here for a long time."

Amy's words gave Daniel a sudden idea. "Don't you have any deeds for the house, Aunt Jill? It must be pretty old if our great, great grandmother lived here. Maybe it's listed or something."

He didn't know *exactly* what that meant, but he'd heard his dad discuss that kind of thing with his mum when they moved some years before. He knew from a school project that some old buildings in his town were 'listed,' which usually meant they couldn't be changed. And he was pretty sure they especially couldn't be knocked down.

"The man asked me that question." His aunt smiled at him. "But he probably hoped I didn't have any. I know the house is very old, but I haven't a clue where the deeds and all that kind of thing are kept. My own mother and father never lived here. I do remember Gran once saying the papers were supposed to be in the house somewhere, but she couldn't find them before she died. She never seemed worried about them though. When she left the cottage to me, the lawyer had the will and let me know about it."

"Maybe that's where the deeds are," Daniel suggested.

"Mm, don't think so," Aunt Jill said. "He's been the family lawyer for years and he said it was just a formality handing over the cottage to me. In fact, come to think of it, he seemed surprised there weren't any other papers. Of course, it didn't matter to me at the time. I didn't need anything else as long as Amy and I could live here."

Daniel wondered if all the women in the family had been as engrossed in their painting as Aunt Jill, apart from his mum. Maybe none of them bothered with practical things like deeds. Although he guessed Amy might be different, since she wanted to travel.

"Anyway, let's not think about all that just now," said Aunt Jill. "The man's not coming back with more details until after the New Year. You two can have a search of the cottage, if you like, see if you can find the papers."

Gosh, how quickly his aunt pushed the problem away and became happy again, Daniel thought. His mum would have worried and bothered about something like this for days, or weeks even.

Even Amy seemed happy to forget about the proposed destruction for now. Daniel had a sinking feeling he knew why.

"Let's do a wee bit more of the jigsaw, Daniel," Amy insisted. "I can't wait to see if anything else happens."

"I hope it doesn't." Although not so keen to do any more, he was curious, too, still not believing anything could *really* change.

They sat at the living room table again and checked over the parts of the jigsaw picture they'd completed, comparing it with the lid.

"Yes, see." Daniel pointed to the flowering bush. "That's like the one near the sundial!"

Amy shrugged. "Why don't we do the top next, then we can get the sky done before the house, that should be safe enough."

"The whole thing's too weird and unlikely, Amy. Imagine a jigsaw picture turning into a real place. That's not possible."

They took most of the day to do the sky as the pieces of blue and white were so fiddly and almost identical. Then they completed it right down to the top of the house.

"We've got to do at least one of the windows," Amy said, getting excited. "Just one, Daniel."

He gave in, again. They'd just started the first grey bits of house when they heard Aunt Jill call down.

"I'll be down in a minute for some lunch, kids, have a look in the fridge and see what you want."

Daniel stood up right away, still not sure about completing the jigsaw house.

"Oh, great, we'll need to leave it till later I suppose," Amy grumped.

Aunt Jill talked a little more about the problem with the new road. "You know, I don't think they can just cut right through the woods. That area might be protected because of the wildlife or something. And they're not allowed to cut down trees nowadays."

Daniel nodded. He'd heard that, too. But what if the council already had permission?

"We'll have to try to find the deeds as soon as possible," Amy said.

Daniel agreed. It might be good fun looking for them, like a treasure hunt.

As soon as lunch was over, he turned to Amy. "Why don't we go and start the search of the house now? We could leave the jigsaw till tomorrow, then we'll be able to compare the cottage in daylight as we finish it."

He was surprised when Amy agreed at once. Maybe she was getting a bit freaked by the jigsaw as well and simply pretended there was nothing strange about it. Anyway, they had to save the cottage, so they might as well begin the search right away.

And they could leave the strange jigsaw for another while.

Chapter Five

Amy immediately took charge.

"Well, the obvious place to start must be the kitchen drawers because they were here before we came," she said. "Then we can check all the cupboards down here and upstairs."

Daniel went along with it since it was her house, and she knew where they could look. They had good fun rummaging through all the messy drawers and finding lots of odds and ends. String, sticky tape, scissors, a few screwdrivers, old plugs, two small paintbrushes, a train timetable, and other things he didn't recognise. But nothing that looked anything like deeds for a house.

They even pulled the drawers right out to check nothing had fallen down the back of them, but found no papers squashed behind. They did the same with the old sideboard in the sitting room, and then an ancient tallboy in the spare room where Daniel was sleeping.

"That's all the old pieces of furniture we found in the house when we moved in," Amy said at last. "That just leaves the attic, Daniel. Let's go and explore." She ran up the stairs to get the ladder down for the attic.

Where did she get all the energy? They'd been searching for ages and Daniel already felt tired. But he'd have to keep up or Amy would tease him.

Once they'd climbed into the attic, Daniel saw the room seemed quite big and was completely floored with wood so they could safely stand inside. It even had a light, but junk covered nearly every part of the floor.

"This is going to take some time. Maybe we should come back another day," Daniel said hopefully.

"Aw, come on, Daniel, let's start now. It's not *that* late."

Somehow, he knew her answer before Amy replied. They'd just have to get it searched as quickly as possible.

Picking up the biggest items from the floor and leaving them to one side helped them walk about more easily. Daniel noticed a small rocking horse, an old school desk, and a long rolled up carpet right in the middle.

"Nearly all of this belonged to Mum's grandmother and great grandmother, so the papers could be anywhere. Mum hasn't got around to looking at everything yet," Amy said.

Daniel guessed his Aunt Jill probably didn't get around to attending to much apart from painting and illustrating books. She was really cool, though, and he could understand why she got so absorbed.

They looked inside the desk first and then searched through some cases and trunks they found at one end. Apart from old clothes and photographs, they contained nothing of real interest, although one of the black and white photos caught Daniel's attention.

"Hey, look, Amy. This must be our great, great grandmother from the really old-fashioned way she's dressed. Can we take this downstairs?"

Amy barely paused in her search. "If you like old photos, you might as well."

Guessing Amy couldn't care less, Daniel pushed the photo into his pocket. He'd study it properly later.

They carried on, peering into all the nooks and crannies of the room, shifting things out of the way when necessary. Then Daniel looked up and saw it.

"Hey look at this, Amy."

An old grandfather clock stood propped up in the farthest corner. When they reached it, the thick dust covered it so completely they could hardly make out the pattern on the clock face.

Daniel wiped it with his sleeve. The face seemed faded as though worn away with standing there too long. He tried to move the stiff hands but they were stuck. Then he noticed two keyholes without a key. It wouldn't work if it needed winding up. He tugged at the door casing for ages to get it open.

"Och, that's not much use if it doesn't work, is it?" Amy asked impatiently.

But Daniel tried again and suddenly he managed to open the long, creaky, wooden door below the clock face a tiny bit, enough to see the huge pendulum that hung motionless below the face.

"See, I told you that's no use," Amy said scornfully. "Come on, we're nearly finished searching."

Daniel was about to answer, but when he drew in his breath to speak he coughed instead as he closed the pendulum door. He stood up straighter, gasping a bit. Not much air up here.

"The door too heavy for you?" asked Amy sweetly.

"No, of course not! It's the dust up here that's making me…cough…but, I'm not wheezing yet."

"Oops, sorry, forgot about that. Well, I don't think we're ever going to find any papers up here anyway," Amy announced and made her way to the stairs. "Are you coming or are you going to stay here until you do wheeze?"

"Thanks for being so concerned!" Daniel said.

When Amy laughed, Daniel realised he was getting as sarcastic as his cousin. He brushed as much dust away as possible. After a last glance at the attic, he followed Amy down the ladder. Thankfully, he started to breathe easier once they were downstairs. He felt for his inhaler. Where had he put it? He searched in his pockets. Not there. Still must be in his jacket.

Daniel went straight to the jacket he had on earlier and found the inhaler in the pocket. He sprayed one puff into his mouth and began to feel much better when his airways opened and he could breathe easier. He'd need to remember to keep it with him all the time.

Later, they had a closer look at the old photo of an elderly woman sitting very upright in an uncomfortable looking chair.

"She looks a bit like some of the paintings of Queen Victoria, doesn't she?" Amy asked.

Daniel nodded as he stared at the long black dress and frilled bonnet tied under the chin with ribbons. But the woman's face held his attention. "Don't you think she has a kind face?" he asked Amy. "Look, it's as though she's smiling right at us."

He heard Amy snort with laughter. "Och, Daniel, it's only an old photo. She's staring at whoever took the photo. And come to think of it, I didn't know they could take photos in those days."

No matter what Amy said, he had the feeling the old lady smiled at *him*. Then he heard Amy's last remark.

"Must've been taken when the new photography became more popular."

Not that he knew much about it, but Amy seemed suitably impressed.

"Anyway, you can keep the photo," Amy added and glanced at Daniel. "D'you want to do some more of the jigsaw?"

He half expected that and was as curious as Amy to see what would happen when they finished the jigsaw house.

"Okay, I suppose we could maybe put in a few more pieces."

They started with the grey house bits again. This time they completed the upper crisscross windows before Aunt Jill remembered it was well past their bed time and came looking for them.

"We just want to finish this last wee bit for tonight," Amy pleaded with her mum.

"As long as it's only another five minutes. Remember, you're staying up late tomorrow night." His aunt left them to it and went through to clear up the kitchen.

They were determined to finish the windows before going to look outside again.

"We're nearly there," Amy broke their concentration and picked out the last few pieces of lead and glass patterned puzzle and fitted them into place.

"What about the door?" she asked.

"No!" Daniel stood up. "Let's go and see the back of the cottage now. I want to prove that weird things like this can't happen in real life before we do the last bit."

The kitchen was empty so they guessed Aunt Jill had gone back upstairs. They put all the lights on and hurried out the back door. Amy and Daniel slowly turned round. And gasped. All the upper back windows were just like the ones in the jigsaw. Old-fashioned and crisscrossed.

"I-I don't like this anymore," Amy said. "This can't really happen. Are we dreaming?"

"There's only one way to find out if it's real, I guess. We have to finish the whole jigsaw and see what happens then." Daniel hoped he sounded braver than he felt.

They went back to the table and shuffled through what was left of the pieces.

"That's weird." Daniel stared at some of the wooden shapes and colours. "These look like pieces of people. But there aren't any figures in the picture on the box, and look, there seems to be space for them beside the door."

"Don't put them in Daniel. I'm beginning to get a horrible feeling about this," said Amy. "Maybe we should tell Mum." Amy sat in thought for a moment. "Let's wait and tell her tomorrow, once we finish it all."

Daniel was happy to agree. The whole thing was definitely stranger than before, but he still didn't believe the house would really change. Yet how could the windows be different? He'd never looked at them properly before they started the jigsaw. Maybe Amy was winding him up, and there had always been some older windows at the back of the house.

He put the remaining pieces down on the table, but he'd made a decision. They had to know for sure if there was something strange about the jigsaw puzzle, or if it was just their wild imagination.

Chapter Six

"Let's go for a walk and explore the woods since they might not be here much longer," Amy said as soon as they'd finished breakfast. She didn't mention the jigsaw and Daniel was happy to go for a walk. He wanted to explore a bit more of the area.

It looked dry and frosty outside so they wrapped up in heavy jackets and scarves. Daniel slung his new binoculars around his neck as they set off toward the woods. They tramped through the overgrown paths and ancient trees for a while, not saying a word to each other for ages. Daniel was sure Amy thought about the jigsaw, same as him.

"Ever think the trees are kind of creepy when so many of them are bare at this time of year?" Daniel eventually asked.

"Never thought about it," Amy replied. "They're just trees without leaves."

Daniel sighed. Amy had no imagination at all. They tramped on a little farther, no sound apart from an occasional bird and their own breathing.

"It'll be great to stay up late tonight," Daniel broke the silence. "What do you actually *do* on Hogmanay?"

"Have you never done *anything*?" Amy teased. "When it gets late we put the television on for the party programme, and we dance about to the Scottish music. Then we eat some sultana cake and shortbread and drink ginger wine. When it's midnight we wish each other Happy New Year."

Maybe Amy was kidding about the dancing, but the rest sounded okay. Daniel thought about his mum and dad, wondering where they were now. What would they be doing at midnight? It would be a different time in America from midnight in Scotland.

He felt guilty he wasn't missing them so much now, because of the jigsaw and Amy and the house and everything, but his mum would be glad if she knew. He grinned at his cousin. She really wasn't bad for a girl, though he missed his friend, Paul, sometimes. But wait till he told him about the jigsaw. As if there really was anything to tell.

It was great walking through the woods, and he wondered what it would be like being on a real adventure, tracking wildlife. Did anything actually live here? Obviously, there wouldn't be any *real* wildlife, like bears, or wolves, or anything. But he remembered reading about the big wildcats that sometimes lived in the north of Scotland. Maybe they weren't far enough north there. Foxes! That was a possibility, though they wouldn't come out when people were about. And there wasn't near enough water for otters. Maybe some owls flew about the woods at night.

As they came to a clearer area, Daniel suddenly stopped.

"Look, Amy." He bent down on one knee making Amy nearly fall over him.

"What now?" she grumbled. "It's too cold to kneel down on the ground."

"I think this might be a rare plant. I've never actually seen a real one before, but I'm sure it's like the one we were doing a project on in school a while ago. I can't remember its name—wintergreen or something, maybe."

"You a plant expert, are you? It looks like a lot of leaves to me. Anyway, so what? You're not allowed to pick it or anything, so what're you so excited about?" Amy asked.

"I know that. But, if there's a rare plant here, then the woods can't be destroyed. Aunt Jill would have to get someone to check for sure."

"Oh, right. Once they know about it, I expect everyone in the village will want to save the woods," Amy eventually added.

She was silent for a while as they walked on. Daniel hoped she was impressed by his knowledge. He looked sideways at her and she suddenly grinned.

"Let's go back home," she said, "We've had enough exercise, and it's freezing out here. I've changed my mind about not doing the jigsaw. I'm dying to get on with it now."

Daniel sighed. He enjoyed looking for plants and things, but half his mind was still on the jigsaw, too.

They turned back the way they'd come. Then Daniel stopped again to peer through the binoculars.

"Not another plant," Amy sounded bored now.

"No, listen. Can you hear that noise? Listen...click, click...it's getting quicker, and wait, there it is—a sound like a cork being pulled from a bottle." Daniel was getting excited. "I think it's a capercaillie. They're quite rare you know."

"A what?" Amy sounded even more bored.

"A capercaillie. It's a bit like a black grouse except when it's flying you can see the tail is more rounded. It's sometimes called the horse of the woods. Quick, take the binoculars." He shoved them at Amy and pointed to the sky where the trees were less crowded. Birds *were* something he knew a lot about.

"I see them. I see them," Amy sounded nearly as excited. "There're two of them, one dark and one a bit lighter. Here." She gave back the binoculars and Daniel watched the male and female bird fly off into the distance.

"They must be nesting around here. There're probably lots of good tree roots for them. Hope we haven't scared them away. Well that does it, we definitely need to get someone to come and check out the woods. If there are rare plants and birds then they haven't a hope of wrecking the place."

Amy looked as pleased as him, but then she frowned. "But what about the cottage, Daniel? What if we never find the deeds? I might lose my home."

"We'll just have to search all over again straight after the New Year. And your mum can check with the lawyer. They have to be *somewhere*." He was determined to find them before he went back home. He didn't want Amy and his aunt to lose their home. Apart from them having to find a new place to live, the cottage was a great place to come and stay for a visit.

As soon as they got home, they had one thought.

"Right," Amy said at once, "let's get this jigsaw finished and prove it's just a picture."

Daniel was glad Amy felt the same as him. They *had* to complete it now. No matter what happened.

Chapter Seven

"See I told you, those pieces look like people," Amy said. Odd bits of puzzle lay on the table with the exact space left for them in the jigsaw.

They put all the extra pieces in place at the door of the jigsaw house. The puzzle was finished and every space filled. Two figures stood in front of the jigsaw house door, but there were no figures on the box picture.

"Weirder and weirder," Amy whispered. "What do we do now?"

Daniel heard the fear in her voice. "We break the whole thing up and put it back in the box?" he suggested, hoping she'd agree, but at the same time wanting to see what would happen next.

"I think we should get something to eat first. I'm hungry after all that walking in the woods," Amy said. As she stood up, she knocked the empty jigsaw box on to the floor. She bent down to pick it up then noticed a piece of paper sticking out of the inside corner.

"Daniel. I think you'd better have a look at this."

Wondering why Amy sounded so strange, Daniel glanced at the hand she held out. He took the sheet of paper from her and stared, trying to understand what it said. It had some kind of rhyme written on it, in flowing, old-fashioned handwriting.

For a moment he wondered if Amy had put it on the floor to tease him. Then he noticed the expression on her face.

"It was sticking out of the box lid when it fell," Amy said quietly.

They spread the paper on the table, sat down and examined it carefully. Unusual dark writing was scrawled across the page.

Make the jigsaw piece by piece,
It will lead you to great deeds.
When shadows fall on passing years,
Take courage in the midst of fears.
Be strong of heart and calm of mind,
If past and present be combined.
The key to secrets held through time
Is found in wood and ringing chime.

"This is even weirder," Daniel said. "It's actually telling us to make the jigsaw, as though someone knew we'd find this one day. Maybe we were supposed to find it at the beginning, when we opened the box. You said it seemed to be stuck."

Amy nodded. "Even stranger," she said, "is the way it talks about 'great deeds.' Is that the deeds we're looking for or does it mean like great things? You know? It was obviously written a long time ago when people talked about doing deeds."

"Who cares about that?" Daniel asked. "It's the parts about 'courage in the midst of fears' and 'past and present be combined' that I don't like. I mean, what on earth is it all supposed to mean?"

Amy stood up. "As if the jigsaw wasn't strange enough. Now it looks as if there's another puzzle attached to it. Well I say we go and get that drink and something to eat before we decide what to do next."

They raided the fridge and took a drink and some cheese and biscuits back into the living room. Instead of going to the table, Amy switched on the television and they sat down to watch it.

Daniel was relieved to have a rest from thinking about puzzles. Inky came and perched on his knee, while Spicy played around and under the table the jigsaw sat on.

They were laughing at an old cartoon when Daniel began to cough. Then his chest tightened. Soon, he was beginning to wheeze. Trying to get a breath, he pushed Inky off his knee and stood up. Maybe the cat's fur made him cough. He managed to get his inhaler out, while Amy jumped up wondering what to do.

"Will I get Mum?" she asked, trying not to panic.

Daniel shook his head and pushed down the button on the inhaler. He breathed in the spray and then did the same again. His breathing slowed a little and he relaxed.

"It's okay," he said after a few minutes. As he put the inhaler on the table, Daniel noticed Amy's expression. "Don't look so worried. It's not as bad as it used to be. The doctor thinks I might be growing out of it."

Amy half-smiled and shrugged. "It must be the cats—maybe you're allergic to their fur." She put the animals outside the room and shut the door.

"Could be the cartoons," Daniel said. "Laughing too much sometimes makes it worse." He nearly laughed again at the disbelieving expression on Amy's face. But it was true, laughter always made him wheeze, though not as bad as this time.

"So, what now?" Amy asked, trying not to look at the jigsaw, and the cream-coloured piece of paper lying on the table beside it, but unable to help herself. "Let's look at the rhyme again," Amy suggested. "We've decided deeds could mean two things. What about, 'shadows fall on passing years'? Could that mean the sundial? That's how it works, with the sun's shadow falling on it. That's where the key could be, whatever that's for."

Daniel nodded in agreement, but it didn't sound quite right. "I suppose it could be, though why doesn't it mention the sun? I don't think it means that, Amy. And what's that got to do with past and present being combined? Besides, it's talking about a chime, so that's more like a clock. Maybe we should have checked all the clocks in the house."

"The only old one that might chime is the grandfather clock in the attic, but it was well done-in when we found it. There's no way that's going to be of any use." Amy sighed. "And why should we need courage? Or does that just mean we have to finish the jigsaw?"

Daniel stood up, tired of thinking about it. "Who knows? It's all weird. I don't like the way the jigsaw is a bit different from the picture now. I mean, where did the pieces come from to make those two figures? Why are they not on the picture?"

They stood and looked at the completed jigsaw, undecided about what to do next.

"Oh come on, we both want to find out what'll happen next. We have to go outside and have a look at the whole house." Daniel did his best to sound brave. They'd have to go outside eventually.

"Maybe we should break it all up and put it back in the box," Amy said at last.

"Not now after all that work. I think we should go outside and see if anything else has happened first.

There must be some reason why there's a rhyme with the jigsaw." Daniel pushed the paper with the rhyme into his pocket. His hand touched something else. He still had the photo of their great, great grandmother. He glanced at the old photo again and paused. This time he was convinced the old woman smiled at him. Shaking his head at the idea, he stuffed it back in his pocket. No way was he suggesting anything else to Amy.

They slowly walked out the back of the house and closed the door. They stood staring at it. There it was—the strange old-fashioned door knocker from the jigsaw. Like an ugly face. Like in his dream. Daniel knew it couldn't be a mistake, or a joke, this time. The door had definitely changed.

Then they looked at each other, and he gulped.

"Amy, it's us...the figures in the jigsaw, it's us! I-I think we'd better get back inside."

They opened the door, stepped inside the house and stopped dead. Everything had changed.

Chapter Eight

"What's happened to the kitchen?" Amy's voice ended on a squeak.

The modern kitchen appliances like the washing machine and electric cooker had vanished. Now it looked exactly like a very old cottage kitchen from an older time. Big black and copper pans hung from the ceiling and a long, black cooking range stood against one wall. They wandered around the room in a daze, staring at every thing, touching it. It was real. Daniel thought he could even hear a bubbling sound from the old steam kettle on the range, as though water boiled. But it was cold to touch and he couldn't see any steam rising.

They stared at each other and then they made a dash for the living room, hoping everything else looked the same as usual. They almost fell over each other as they came to a sudden halt. Once again, everything was completely different from before. It wasn't Amy's house. At least, Daniel noticed the rooms seemed to be in the same place but nothing else looked familiar. No modern furniture or electric fire, no television, no carpets. Instead, the room had old-fashioned armchairs and a big coal fire grate. A large rug covered some of the wooden floorboards. An old, brown upright piano took up one corner.

They turned and rushed upstairs, calling as they went. "Mum!"

"Aunt Jill!"

No answer. They opened one door after another. No one there, not even the cats. And every single room was as old-fashioned as the downstairs rooms. In the main bedroom, Daniel thought he could smell some kind of sweet, flowery scent.

Then Amy sniffed. "Lavender. Where's that from? I think I can smell lavender. Oh, Daniel, what's happening…" she broke off in a sob.

"Quick, we have to get back outside again," Daniel grabbed Amy's arm. "We'll probably find everything's back to normal again when we go out, then back in." He hoped he was right. He couldn't bear to think what might happen next if they didn't get back to the present.

They ran to the back door. It opened! They could get outside. They walked right around the outside of the cottage. It really did look old-fashioned, like the one in the jigsaw picture, with the same door knocker and crisscross window panes. They hurried around again to the back door. It still stood open and they hesitated.

"We can't stay out here all night, Amy, and we have to get back to your house and Aunt Jill somehow. Come on, maybe it's all some weird blip and everything is back to normal," Daniel said.

"What if it's not?" Amy asked. Daniel didn't answer. He had no idea.

Taking hands, they stepped inside the kitchen again.

Still the old-fashioned kitchen. Then the door banged shut behind them. Daniel turned quickly and tried to open it. Stuck fast. He pushed and pulled and turned the handle. Nothing worked.

"Daniel. I'm really f-frightened. What's *happening*?"

"Oh, Amy, I don't know how, but I think we're inside the house in the jigsaw puzzle." As he said the words, he still couldn't believe it. No way! But he couldn't think of another explanation.

Daniel tried to keep calm for Amy's sake, though he felt like crying. He'd never see his mother and father or his friends ever again and they'd never know what had happened to him. Then he remembered all those dreams. He was inside that same house, but he'd never seen how the dreams ended.

He wondered where Aunt Jill was right now, if she would even notice they were missing. Maybe not until midnight. Anyway, what could she do? Break the jigsaw? Then they might disappear forever. He gulped at the thought. They were trapped inside an empty, very old house and right now there seemed to be no way to get out.

Chapter Nine

They ran through the house again, checking the other door and all the windows. Nothing would open. Daniel's heart beat faster. His face started to get all hot and sweaty. Then his chest tightened. Difficult to get breath… He gasped a few times, trying to suck in some air. He needed his inhaler.

He put his hand in his pocket. It wasn't there! He searched the other pocket. Same thing. Then he remembered. He'd put it on the table in the real house during that asthma attack while watching the cartoons.

He started to breathe even quicker, panic taking over at not having his inhaler. Daniel leaned against the wall, half-bent over, gasping for another breath. He was going to die here! And Amy would be all alone, trapped in a house that didn't exist like this any more.

Then Amy grabbed his hand. She stared wildly at him. He could see her horrified panic. Daniel calmed down a little bit, trying to remember what he should do. He began to take slow deep breaths like he'd once been shown by the doctor. And he squeezed Amy's hand.

Gradually, his breathing became quieter. He wiped the sweat from his brow. As his breath came back to normal, something made him stand up straighter while he tried to remember.

The rhyme. Pulling it from his pocket, he read, '*Be calm of mind.*' How strange. And he really worked hard to stay calmer.

"You okay, Daniel? Where's your inhaler? Please don't give me any more frights!" Amy scolded, though she patted his arm in relief.

"I'll be fine." Since his voice sounded almost normal again, he didn't want to tell her he'd stupidly left the inhaler behind. That might freak her out even more.

"What are we going to do, Daniel? We're trapped…"

When he heard the rising panic in her voice again, it kept him calmer.

"There *must* be a way out, Amy. Things like this just don't happen. There's got to be a window open somewhere. We can try, and at least it's something to do."

They hurried through each room trying to open the windows. Every one stayed tightly shut. They couldn't see any way to get them opened. Unless they tried to break one? Daniel wondered.

"Look for something heavy," he told Amy. "We might be able to break a window."

They searched in each of the bedrooms but couldn't see anything heavy enough to smash the glass, yet light enough to lift. Daniel ran downstairs to the kitchen. Surely must be something there. He opened every single cupboard, rummaging through their contents.

The only possibility was some kind of wrench-type thing he found in one cupboard.

He ran back upstairs. Amy hadn't found anything suitable.

"Stand back. Let me try this," Daniel said. He raised back the arm holding the wrench and swung it at the window, bracing himself for a loud smash and breaking glass. Nothing happened.

"Oh no, nothing we do is going to work!" Amy cried.

Daniel couldn't understand it. The doors and windows didn't work, yet he could sniff faint smells of cooking food, like…boiled cabbage. As though someone was cooking in the kitchen, yet no one was in the house. The house was lit up as though lamps were switched on somewhere, so at least they weren't in total darkness.

"Let's bang on the window," Daniel suggested. The cottage didn't sit near any other houses, so probably no one would hear them. If anyone was out there at all in this weird other place. But it was something else to do.

They stood at a bedroom window, banging and shouting as hard and loud as they could.

No use. They really were still trapped.

"But who lives here?" asked Amy. "And where are they?"

Daniel shrugged. "Well, the house used to belong to Aunt Jill's great grandmother, so maybe this is what it looked like when she lived here. And maybe she used lavender scent and cooked cabbage on that kitchen range."

Amy glanced at him. "You can smell it, too? I thought I was imagining it."

"But I don't know why there's nobody here," Daniel said. "Unless, maybe we're in a kind of time warp. You know, like a parallel universe, but without the people who used to live here."

"A what?" Amy looked at him as if he'd grown another head.

"You know—two places in the universe that exist at the same time."

He suddenly stopped talking.

"What? What is it?"

Amy looked puzzled as he pulled the piece of paper from his pocket.

"Listen! 'When shadows fall on passing years, take courage in the midst of fears. Be strong of heart and calm of mind, if past and present be combined.' That's what's happening, past and present *are* combined. It's coming true, Amy, the rhyme does mean something!"

The only problem being he still didn't know exactly what it all meant. And how would it help them to escape? They were stuck here in another time, maybe another dimension, and right now there seemed no way to get back to where they should be. Daniel tried not to show his fear, but he was running out of ideas.

"Let me see the last part again," Amy said, grabbing the paper.

'The key to secrets kept through time, is found in wood and ringing chime.'

"Well, that's a great help… I don't think," she complained, handing it back.

"Let's have another look downstairs," Daniel suggested. He thought he could hear a faint echo of piano music but didn't want to scare Amy again.

They trudged back down the stairs and searched again in all the rooms for some signs of life. Creepily, it was as if no one had ever lived in the house at all. Yet Daniel could hear something else. A very faint sound, unless he imagined it. But not piano music this time.

"Can you hear that, Amy?" Daniel paused in the living room. It sounded almost like voices. Only not quite. As though someone whispered from a long way off.

"What? I can't hear anything. You're scaring me, Daniel."

"It's okay, Amy. Wishful thinking for a moment, or too much imagination. There's nothing here."

So Amy couldn't hear anything. But Daniel was sure he heard the echo of someone from the past. Maybe from the people who actually lived in the old house, maybe his great, great grandmother? He pulled out the old photo and stared at the now familiar-looking face.

He looked up and saw the same face smiling from a framed drawing on the wall.

"Look," he nudged Amy. "It's great, great grandmother."

"What?" Amy swung round to where he pointed, terror in her voice. "Daniel! You really scared me there. I thought she was standing in the room with us."

"Sorry." He hadn't thought of that. "But see, she looks the same as in this old photo, and she's definitely smiling at us. I think it's her memories that are all around us." He could see Amy thought he was losing it, and he decided not to tell her more of his weird ideas.

Maybe great, great grandmother *was* alive in this parallel universe and could almost hear him and Amy. But he couldn't try and explain that to his cousin when he hardly understood it himself. She'd really freak out if he started talking about ghostly presences, though it didn't frighten him for some reason.

They dragged their feet back upstairs again and looked in every room once more. As if it was likely that anything would suddenly change. The bedrooms each had a neatly made bed covered with a warm-looking patchwork quilt. Daniel looked at them longingly. He couldn't care less about staying up for New Year's any more. He just wanted to climb into his bed at Aunt Jill's and pretend this was all a nightmare. He even noticed one of the rooms had a very slight smell of paint.

"Oh, this is no use." Amy stood on the landing. "We're never going to get back, Daniel. I'm tired and cold. I want my mum. I wish we'd never started the stupid jigsaw!"

Daniel could hear the same fear in Amy's voice that he felt inside. What were they going to do? Would someone find their skeletons one day and wonder who they were? What about his mum and dad? They were coming to take him home soon. What would they do? And surely even Aunt Jill must have noticed they were missing by now.

He looked at his watch. It still seemed to be working. It was twenty minutes to twelve at night, on the thirty-first of December, in the twenty-first century. His first Hogmanay, staying up to see in the New Year, and they were stuck in a house that looked as if it belonged in the nineteenth century. A whole lot of firsts, and it might also be his last if they didn't escape.

He began to think they might as well give up. They were never going to get back. They'd tried everything they could think of and nothing made any difference.

Amy sat down on the upstairs landing, leaning against the wall. Daniel wasn't sure whether she was crying quietly or if she'd fallen asleep. She'd drawn up her knees and folded her arms across them, resting her head on top.

Daniel sat down beside her. Maybe they should go and lie down on one of the empty beds and hope it *was* just a nightmare. He put his arm around Amy and snuggled close. She moved slightly so she leaned against him.

Then as he looked up from his watch again, he suddenly saw it. The grandfather clock. It stood solidly facing them on the other side of the landing. Daniel sat and stared at it for a minute. He couldn't believe they'd been running past without noticing it until now. It definitely looked like the same one they'd found in the attic. So this must be where it used to stand years ago.

It looked much newer and shinier as there wasn't any dust or grime covering it. Even from where he sat, Daniel could see a pattern on the clock face. He watched it for a few moments, hoping it would do something. No movement. Maybe it didn't work because they were in this strange time warp, yet his watch still showed the passing time.

The more Daniel stared at the clock, the more he knew it was significant in some way. Maybe because of all that talk about parallel universes. Then he thought of the rhyme.

He took the paper from his pocket and read it again.

'The key to secrets kept through time'.

That could definitely mean a clock. But was the key a real key, or did it just mean the answer to something—or both?

'Is found in wood and ringing chime.'

Well, the clock casing was wooden. Did a grandfather clock chime? Yes, he was sure they did, sometimes anyway. So the answer *could* be in the clock.

He stood up and moved quietly away from Amy to have a closer look at the silent grandfather clock.

The time hadn't moved on since he'd noticed it about five minutes ago. He tried to open the long case beneath the face. It was stuck. His nails weren't strong enough to grasp the thin edge. Then he remembered the wrench. It had a thin metal end. Maybe he could force it open with that.

Leaving Amy dozing, he found the wrench and managed to insert the thin end into the edge of the door casing. It gave slightly and he twisted the wrench a little. Next minute, the casing opened completely and he could see inside. The great hanging pendulum hung still. So that obviously wasn't working.

He thought it a brilliant clock, though, definitely made out of dark wood. The face had been painted in green and pink, with the passage of time marked out in Roman numerals.

Two other circular dials completed the centre of the face. One was below the XII for twelve o'clock and the other just below that, above the VI for six o'clock. They had tiny hands on them, too, so they must be for showing the minutes and seconds. It was really cool, Daniel decided, and it stopped him feeling frightened for a while. Even the name, a grandfather clock, made him think of great, great grandmother and her kind face. This must have been her clock.

Then he noticed a name written in fancy writing on either side of the dials. One was next to the IX for nine o'clock, and the other next to the III for three o'clock. He could only read one of the names. It said Ayrshire. That was in Scotland! It must have been made there, in his own country. Then he saw the four o'clock was shown as IIII. He'd always thought Roman numerals depicted a four as IV. Maybe it was a mistake. Or maybe they used to be made that way.

Then he noticed again the two small key holes just above the seconds hand dial, at either side. The clock maybe just needed winding. But where was the key?

Chapter Ten

"Daniel, what're you doing?" Amy's sleepy voice came closer.

"I'm wondering about the grandfather clock. You know? The rhyme and its reference to a key, time, and chime. It's not working and there're *two* key holes. Look."

Amy rubbed her eyes and stared at the clock for a while.

"Did you notice the whole clock's in the shape of a keyhole?" she asked.

Daniel stood back and stared. He'd been so busy looking at the face and dials that he'd never noticed.

"You're right, Amy. That's really strange."

"So it would definitely make sense if the rhyme was something to do with this. But where's the key?"

"It says, 'the key is found in wood and ringing chime.'"

Daniel thought for a few moments. "Well the clock's casing is made of wood." He ran his hand all down the front of the casing, though he could hardly reach the top. Then he looked all down both sides. Nothing there.

"Help me move it from the wall, Amy. Maybe the key's attached to the back."

They eased the heavy clock away from the wall a bit, enough for him to look behind it.

"No, nothing there." His shoulders sagged with disappointment.

They carefully stood the clock back against the wall. He was sure they'd been going to find a small key to fit the locks.

"There's only the top left but I need something to stand on, I can't quite reach." He was a little taller than Amy.

They dragged a chair from the nearest room and Daniel climbed up. The wood at the top of the clock was carved in a swirly pattern. It didn't look like there was anywhere to put a key. He slid his fingers all along the top of the casing. There *was* a flat ledge, but empty. So that was the end of that great idea—no key.

"Why don't you try inside the casing?" Amy suggested.

"Might as well." Daniel opened the long, front wooden door again.

The pendulum and chain just hung there, like in the attic that day. He reached inside, careful to avoid banging against the pendulum. Nothing lay on the floor of the casing.

He stretched up the left side, nothing. Moving his hand up the right side, he touched something. Something metal. He couldn't see properly, but it felt like a tiny hook. He fiddled around a bit. Sure enough, a key was hanging on the hook.

"Found it!" Daniel shouted.

"Brilliant." Amy said, trying to look at the key. Then her smile disappeared as quickly. "The only thing is, how's this going to help us get back?"

"No idea, but at least we can wind the clock up and see what happens, if anything."

Daniel stuck the key in the first hole. It seemed a bit stiff but at least it slowly turned. When he'd finished nothing happened. Then he did the same in the other key hole. As soon as he finished turning the key, they heard it. *"Tick, tock, tick, tock."*

"It's working, the clock's working!" Amy cried.

Then just as suddenly, it stopped again.

"The pendulum isn't moving," Daniel said. "Maybe we need to turn the hands to the right time, or something."

He had no idea how to make it go, but he tried turning the hands on the clock face, moving them clockwise until they read the same time as his watch. Still no tick.

"It must be something to do with the pendulum. It needs to move to keep the time. And there's no chance of any chiming unless it works." Daniel stood back, thought for a moment, and then he slowly tried to push the hanging pendulum and weights. "I think they're stuck." More disappointment.

He tried pushing the pendulum again. Completely stuck. He moved the hands on the clock face. They still moved okay, but the pendulum and weights hung as straight and still as ever.

"There must be something *making* it stick," Amy said crossly. "Anyway, who cares about the stupid clock? I just want to get out of here. What good is a clock that doesn't tell the time? There's no chance it's going to chime."

Daniel ignored her, but she'd given him an idea. Maybe something *was* making it stick. He pushed his hand in behind the pendulum as far as it would go. Nothing there. Then he moved his hand up toward the top of the long stem. And felt something.

"Amy, come here. I think there's something in here," Daniel shouted.

"So, what's the big deal?" Amy was still in a bad mood.

By this time, he'd wriggled his hand about until he could grasp what felt like paper. He pulled. It was stuck. He couldn't quite get his hand right behind the pendulum.

"Amy, you've got to try and get it, whatever it is. Your hands are smaller. Here, stand on the chair and try to get a good hold of it. But watch you don't rip it."

"Might as well, seeing there's nothing else to do." Amy climbed on the chair and reached in and up as far as she could stretch. "I can feel something."

Daniel saw her expression change as she pulled at the paper. She was more interested than she pretended. Finally, she stepped back down, the paper in her hand.

"Let me see!" Daniel tried to take it from her.

"No. I should look first since I got it out."

"Okay," he agreed, "let's look at it together. It's probably a bit of rubbish. Maybe someone just wanted to stop the pendulum from banging about and breaking the wood when the clock moved to the attic."

Spreading the dirty fawn-coloured paper out between them, they stared at the tiny spidery writing. It was too difficult to read. Then Daniel noticed the larger words at the top. Still in strange writing, but he recognised enough letters to guess the rest.

"You know what I think this is, Amy? I think it's the Title Deeds of the house. They've been in the clock all along! That's what the rhyme meant after all."

"Yeah! I think you're right, look you can see the fancy 'D' quite clearly. It *must* be the deeds."

Daniel looked at Amy and then stared at the clock.

"What now? I still don't know how that's going to get us back?" Daniel hated to admit defeat, but couldn't understand what use it was to find the deeds then be stuck here with them.

Then Amy gave a cry that nearly made him jump.

"Daniel, I've just had a horrible thought. What if we don't get back with the deeds and they knock the house down! Where will we be then? Or do we not exist anymore?"

"Oh, Amy, don't say that." He hadn't thought about that possibility. "We're going to get out of here."

"We've *got* to find a way back," Amy said. "The rhyme has been right so far, so the chime bit must mean something."

While Amy sat down and peered at the deeds, trying to make out the rest of the writing, Daniel went back across to examine the clock. How silly, they hadn't tried the pendulum again since removing the paper.

He reached his hand out and gently pushed. It moved! He pushed it harder. And the pendulum swung back and forth. Then he heard the sound again. *"Tick, tock, tick, tock."*

"I think the clock's going again," Daniel called, checking the time on his watch. It was ten minutes to midnight.

Daniel moved the hands of the grandfather clock again until it was exactly the same time as his watch. The pendulum still moved gently back and forth. It was definitely working again. They could still hear the ticking.

"Maybe it's going to chime at midnight," Daniel said in sudden hope, although he couldn't understand what difference it would make.

He flopped back down beside Amy and together they watched the swinging pendulum's hypnotic movement.

Daniel was glad the messing about with the clock had taken their minds off their fear for a while. Now he tried not to think about Amy's words. Could they be destroyed if they didn't escape? Did they still exist at all in this strange parallel world? He had no idea. Maybe they should try praying they'd escape, he wondered. He'd never quite believed if God existed at all. Anyway, where was Heaven? No one had ever seen it and come back to tell people about it.

Then he thought about it. At the moment, he and Amy couldn't be seen by anyone and they still existed. Or he hoped they did. Maybe heaven was like that—in some parallel universe type of place where ordinary people couldn't see it until they died. *No, don't think about dying!* Oh, it was all too confusing. But, it couldn't do any harm, surely. He'd just say the prayer quietly in his head so Amy wouldn't laugh at him.

Dear God, I'm sorry I don't speak to you very much. If you're listening somewhere, could you please make sure we get back home safely? We've done everything we can think of here. The clock's working and we're waiting to see if it chimes. But I don't know how that's going to make any difference. So maybe we could do with your help, too, if you don't mind. Thank you.

It seemed a little silly, as though he was talking quietly to himself. But he felt a tiny bit better since there was nothing else they could do. He listened to the steady *tick, tock, tick, tock*. He took the photo of great, great grandmother from his pocket again. The old lady smiled back at him and a cosy sense of comfort from that kind face warmed his insides.

The ticking clock was another comfort of a sort. "At least something works in this weird, unreal house," he said aloud, just to remind him that he and Amy were still alive.

He'd left the long wooden door of the grandfather clock open and sat watching the pendulum moving back and forth, back and forth. His eyes felt sleepy...

Amy rested her head against his shoulder and they both watched silently, eyes half-closed, as the hands crept toward the twelve o'clock of midnight.

Chapter Eleven

Something had disturbed him.

Daniel couldn't believe he'd actually fallen asleep watching the swinging pendulum. It must have hypnotised them. He rubbed his eyes, hoping everything had been a bad dream, but Amy stirred beside him on the cold landing. She'd been dozing, too.

"Oh no, we're still here," groaned Amy as she opened her eyes. "I thought I'd been dreaming." Then she sat up fully. "Hey, what's that noise?"

Daniel stared at the clock. Then he realised what kind of noise had awakened them.

It was midnight and the clock had started chiming out the hours!

He jumped to his feet as the sound echoed around the empty house. He looked at his watch. It was almost New Year's Day in the real time, too.

"Let's go downstairs," Amy shouted to him. "It's too noisy up here."

As he moved toward the stairs, Daniel heard another sound. The clock was only half-way through the hours. But it wasn't the chimes he heard.

"Listen, Amy, can you hear something? I think there's a noise coming from downstairs." Daniel edged nearer the stairs.

"I think so." Amy stood beside him. "Daniel, I'm scared. What's happening now?"

"Listen—the noise is getting louder." He could definitely hear another sound. Grabbing Amy's hand, they crept to the top stair.

"Daniel! That sounds like cats! Listen, I can hear hissing and yowling, you know, like when they're angry."

He listened carefully. It certainly sounded like cats. But who knew what might happen in this house. Then he listened hard again.

"Amy, you're not going to believe this, but I think I can hear a voice now."

"Mum..."

"Aunt Jill..."

They spoke the words at the same time. And Daniel guessed the same thought was in Amy's mind. Holding hands tightly, they hurried down the stairs, hardly daring to believe what they could hear. They didn't pause or look at anything as they got to the bottom stair. They burst breathlessly into the living room.

"Daniel, Amy, I was wondering where you two had got to. You're nearly missing welcoming in the New Year. Here's a glass of ginger wine for you both."

They stood speechless, staring around the room. It was exactly as they had left it earlier in the evening, before they had completed the jigsaw and went outside. They glanced at each other, unable to move while they tried to work it out.

"What's wrong, are you too tired after all? Did you hear the racket the cats were making? I don't know what got into them tonight. And your poor jigsaw. After all the trouble you've taken!"

Daniel heard his aunt's voice. But it was a few moments before he realised what she was saying.

"Sorry, Aunt Jill, what did you say about the cats?"

"You *are* tired, aren't you? I was saying the cats seemed to go mad this evening. Just as it got to twelve o'clock, they started running all over the place, hissing and spitting. I'm afraid they've spoiled the jigsaw, too. They jumped all over the table and it came apart—just a few minutes before you came downstairs."

Daniel stared at the broken jigsaw. He thought maybe he understood. As much as he ever could, anyway. The cats were now quite happily lying in their usual spot in front of the fire. Could they have heard the chimes of the grandfather clock from the other time? That would be enough to spook them.

Amy hadn't said a word, and Daniel saw her bend down to pick up the jigsaw pieces. She started to put them back into place as though not even thinking about it.

"No! Don't do that Amy!"

As she dropped the piece she had in her hand, Amy looked up as if startled out of a dream. Then she broke up the rest of the jigsaw to put into the box.

Daniel saw his aunt look at him in surprise, and then in even more surprise at Amy obeying him without saying anything.

He shrugged, smiling. "Sorry, I didn't mean to shout, but I think we've had enough of jigsaws."

The rhyme had said the key was found in wood, and they did find it there. But it also said in ringing chime. And the key, the answer, was in the chime. It was only when they found the deeds that it released the pendulum and allowed it to chime. Then that had made the cats go wild, and they'd destroyed the jigsaw.

That must be it. As soon as the jigsaw broke up, they were back in the present. It must have broken the spell. Only one way to find out. They had to go back upstairs. And then they had to go outside the back door and come in again.

Chapter Twelve

"Amy, I think I left something upstairs, can you help me look?"

Daniel nearly laughed at Amy's horrified stare. But he wasn't going back upstairs on his own.

"I suppose so, but hurry up. I want to watch the end of the Hogmanay show on television."

As they went into the hall, Amy stopped him going any farther.

"Are you mad? We don't want to get trapped again!"

"It's okay, I think. Don't you see? I think when the cats destroyed the jigsaw it broke the time spell. We've got to make sure. Anyway, we'll be going upstairs to bed later. Better to find out now."

Slowly, they climbed each stair. Everything seemed as it should be. Then they reached the landing. The grandfather clock had gone.

"See, it *is* back to normal." Now Daniel knew they had to do the next bit.

"We've got to go outside and back in again. That's when it happened the last time, after we'd been outside. We've got to make sure."

"Can you go out and I'll keep watch here?" Amy asked.

"Aye, right!" Then he said quietly, "I can't do it without you, Amy, and remember two figures appeared in the jigsaw."

Amy reluctantly nodded. Daniel didn't blame her as he didn't want to go back outside either. But he wouldn't believe it was over until they did.

"We're just going outside to see the stars," Amy called to Aunt Jill.

"Take a piece of coal with you Daniel, then you can be our First Foot. You're tall, dark and handsome enough!" his aunt called in reply, making Daniel's face heat up with embarrassment and pleasure.

"Not!" Amy added. "Don't want you getting big-headed."

"What's a first foot?" Daniel asked, and why did it matter what he looked like?

"Have you not heard of that Scottish tradition?" Amy asked. "It's supposed to be good luck if the first person over the door at the start of a New Year is a tall, dark, and handsome man. He should bring a gift and it used to be a piece of coal and some shortbread biscuits or cake. We have an electric fire, of course, but people still take something when they visit each other."

"Then I'll take this piece of shortbread out with me and hope we get back in. I suppose we'd better get this over with."

They held hands and Daniel opened the back door. They checked the outside of the door first. It was back to normal. But they still had to go outside. It was the only way to be absolutely sure.

"Here goes." Daniel gripped Amy's hand even tighter, at the same time she squeezed his hard.

They stepped outside. And closed the door. They turned round.

The strange door knocker had gone. So far, so good. Opening the door again, they stepped inside. The modern kitchen units gleamed in the light from the ceiling. It must be true. The broken jigsaw had brought everything back to normal.

"Oh, Daniel, it's over, we're safe again." Amy was nearly sobbing with relief. "And by the way, I really don't think you're that tall and handsome."

Daniel laughed. Amy, too, was back to normal.

"Here, have another glass of ginger wine," Aunt Jill said as they joined her back in the living room. "A Happy New Year, children. Imagine, this might be the last one in this house if we can't find the deeds."

"The deeds!" they both shouted at once.

"Tell Mum, Daniel," Amy said excitedly.

Daniel felt in his two side pockets and knew the colour must be draining from his face. He'd forgotten about the deeds. He didn't have them. He only had the rhyme and the old photo. And they wouldn't be in the clock in the attic anymore. They'd taken them out in that other time. He must have left them there. It was all for nothing.

He was about to tell Amy when he remembered. Amy had been the last person to look at them when trying to read the writing while he was making the clock go again.

"You've got them, Amy, remember?"

Amy shook her head. "No, I gave them back to you once the pendulum was moving again."

"What pendulum?" Aunt Jill stared from one to the other. "What are you talking about? Where did you find the deeds?"

Daniel swallowed. There weren't any deeds again. At least they *might* be lying in some parallel existence, but not here. How silly of them to leave them there. He tried to remember what happened after he saw Amy reading them. Maybe he'd picked them up when they were sitting on the landing floor, before he'd fallen asleep.

He felt in the back pocket of his jeans. Yes! He'd shoved them in just in time.

"We've found them, Aunt Jill." He saw Amy's sigh of relief. "Look, they were inside the grandfather clock all the time."

"Oh, you clever children! So that's what you've been doing all evening, you've been in the attic again. Well done."

Daniel grinned at Amy. Maybe it would be better to keep it their secret for now. No one would believe how they found the deeds anyway.

Then Daniel looked at his Aunt Jill again and wondered. It was something to do with the way she smiled at them. She was an artist like her great grandmother. He thought of his strange dreams. This was *his* great, great grandmother's cottage and she'd painted the jigsaw, and probably wrote the rhyme. And he was hoping to be an artist one day. Did they all have some weird connection with each other down through the years?

He glanced over at Amy who was now playing with the cats while watching the dancing on the television. Maybe Amy was different. She always seemed too practical and didn't seem to like art at all.

Did his aunt just pretend she thought they were in the attic? Maybe they could tell her about it before he went home. Maybe she could explain about the rhyme and tell them more about their great, great grandmother. There was definitely something strange about the way his aunt glanced at them now and then. As though she knew what had happened with the jigsaw. Daniel shrugged. He was probably getting over-imaginative again. And they were safe.

Not long after one o'clock on New Year's morning, Daniel climbed wearily into bed. As he started to fall asleep, he sat up suddenly.

His inhaler! He'd forgotten all about it in the excitement and hadn't even noticed. He wondered what that meant. Maybe he was managing to control his breathing much better. Or maybe the doctor was right, and he was finally growing out of the asthma after all. That would be so cool.

He wondered where his mother and father were right now. Were they missing him? He'd soon find out, for he'd be going home in the next couple of days.

Chapter Thirteen

New Year's Day passed so quickly that Daniel couldn't believe his mum and dad would be home in two days' time. On the second day of January, he and Amy walked through the woods after lunch, planning when he could come back and stay with them.

"You've got to be here when they investigate that bird, the caper...something. You're the one who heard it," Amy said, "so it's only right you should see if it really is that kind."

"The capercaillie." He wasn't going to argue with that idea. Daniel loved Amy's house and the surrounding countryside. He could understand why Aunt Jill and her great grandmother had loved it so much. And he had no fear at all now, even after what happened. He totally thought it was *meant* to happen, so they could save the cottage.

Mum and Dad wouldn't mind at all if he came to stay now and then, and Amy was good fun most of the time. As long as they didn't do any more jigsaws. And he still wanted to see some of Aunt Jill's paintings.

They didn't know what to do with the jigsaw after putting the pieces back in the box.

"Maybe we could give it away to a jumble sale?" Amy suggested.

Daniel shrugged. "I suppose it might only have a spell if someone puts it together in this cottage, as it's the one painted on the lid."

Maybe their great, great grandmother still protected her house and those who loved it down through the years. But he thought the spell, if they could call it that, had been completely broken now.

Next day, Aunt Jill came to find Daniel. "Why don't you come and see some of my paintings. You could even paint one yourself."

"Cool! Would you mind, Amy?" He didn't want to abandon her just before he was going back home.

"'Course not. I'm not interested in painting. I'll watch television while you're in the studio. We can do something later."

The room his aunt used wasn't as big as his bedroom. But a huge window on one side near the ceiling let in lots of light. It looked a bit of a mess, with easels, paintings, brushes, water jars, paint-covered rags, and paint pots all around. But it looked totally brilliant to him. The strong smell of white spirit and paint reminded Daniel of that faint smell of paint in one of the rooms of the old jigsaw cottage. He was pretty sure his great, great grandmother had used this same room for her paintings.

"Here's what I've been working on," Aunt Jill said, gesturing to an easel holding an almost-completed canvas.

Daniel stared at the painting of the woods. The same woods he and Amy had walked through that day. Similar tall, leafless trees reached to the winter sky and beneath them the winding path they'd walked along. He noticed this path seemed slightly different, wider at the beginning before getting narrower as it disappeared into the distance between the trees.

A single figure wandered along the path, carrying something in its hands. Daniel peered closer. It looked like binoculars, like *his* binoculars. But now the picture didn't remind him of that day in the woods with Amy. It seemed more like the one in his dream, when he'd walked through woods just like this. Before he ever came here.

He turned to his aunt. “The woods are going to be saved aren’t they?”

She smiled her knowing smile. “Of course they are, but only because you found the plant and heard the bird call.”

He blinked. Had they told her about that yet? He couldn’t remember. Maybe Amy had told her.

“Why don’t you try painting something, Daniel? Anything you like. You can use this spare easel, there’s some heavy practice paper on it for you. Do you want to try oil paints?”

“Yeah, that would be great, thanks. I’ve never used them before. We only get to paint with water colours at school and I have some at home.” He didn’t tell her he used a kid’s paint box.

“I’m sure you’ll manage fine. Something tells me you’re a natural. Like me, and grandmother, and great grandmother. Sometimes it misses a generation. Or someone gets the gift rather than another person.”

This time, he wondered if she was talking about more than painting. But he wasn’t sure he wanted to know anymore just now. Not yet.

Once he started painting, Daniel couldn’t believe how much fun it was, easier than he’d thought. Aunt Jill helped him get used to making the right size strokes with the thicker paint and left some colours ready mixed for him to use.

Daniel painted two birds in flight across the sky above a bluish-grey loch with the green and purple hills in the background. He felt happier than he’d been for a long time. Maybe *he’d* like living here one day, he decided. He much preferred the countryside to the busy town.

“That’s very good Daniel,” his aunt’s voice broke into his thoughts as she turned from her own painting. “You can do some more pictures any time you come.” He could feel his face grow warm with the praise from Aunt Jill. She looked as if she meant it.

“You love this cottage, too, don’t you?” she asked.

Daniel wondered if she could read his mind. “Yeah, it’s a great place to live.”

“That’s good. I’m glad you think so. I had a feeling you would. Amy’s not really a country person. I think she’ll be off to Glasgow or Edinburgh as soon she gets the chance. Maybe even farther away one day.”

She was probably right. But he wanted to go places someday, too. Either to paint or photograph wild animals. Though it would be good to have somewhere to come back to like this. And if he ever had the chance, the first thing he’d do would be to get the old grandfather clock cleaned up and working again.

He couldn’t believe how long he’d been in the studio, when Aunt Jill told him they’d better think about eating.

Amy! He’d left her on her own all this time. She’d be really annoyed with him.

But when he’d cleaned his hands and went back downstairs, Amy was still engrossed in a television programme. She didn’t even look as if she’d missed him.

“Hi, enjoy your painting then?” Amy asked as Daniel sat down on the other seat.

“Yeah, it was brilliant.” He noticed she was just as absorbed in the programme as he’d been in the painting. They were as bad as each other, only with different things.

The rest of the evening passed quickly by the time they’d eaten and helped to clear up. Since they had no jigsaw to do, they watched a film Daniel had never seen.

It wasn't until he drifted off to sleep that he remembered this was his last night in the cottage. His mum and dad were coming home next day.

Chapter Fourteen

"Daniel! It's time to get up. Daniel! Don't you remember what day this is?"

Slowly, he opened his eyes and saw Amy peering round the door, ready to knock again.

"What? What time is it?"

"Come on sleepyhead, it's nearly ten o'clock. Your mum and dad will be here soon."

When Amy had gone away, he lay for another few minutes. There was something he needed to remember.

That was it. He'd dreamed again last night. Not the same dreams he'd had before. This time, he'd been in some kind of castle. He didn't know if Amy had been with him. But he'd definitely seen a suit of armour and a shield and one of those long things—a lance.

He'd always liked stories about knights and castles, so he'd obviously been dreaming a good dream. Hadn't he? Yet, he wondered, why now? Then he remembered something else. One of his aunt's paintings. He was sure he'd noticed one of a medieval castle and knights jousting. That must be it. He'd seen the painting and it had made him think about castles. That was all it meant.

Daniel quickly washed and dressed. He wanted to finish off his painting before his parents arrived. There was only a little bit left to do. Aunt Jill left him on his own for a while. He had a quick look at the other paintings standing about to see if he could find the one with a castle on it. Nothing at all like that. Strange. Maybe he only thought he'd seen one.

He added the last bit of yellow ochre paint to the birds. Finished! It didn't look too bad he decided and guessed he'd get even better with practice.

After lunch, he had a final walk with Amy.

"So, you'll come back and see us as soon as you've got some time off school?"

"That'd be cool, thanks. And you've got to let me know what happens with the woods and the cottage."

"'Course I will, you're the one who saved them—we hope!"

Daniel hoped he did see Amy again soon. He'd become fond of her and she wasn't nearly so bossy now, after their scary time in the old cottage.

In the middle of the afternoon, they heard a car arrive. His parents were home!

He ran out to meet them but stopped suddenly, surprised to see a taxi. He was even more surprised when only his mum got out and paid the driver. Then the taxi drove away.

"Daniel, love, it's so good to see you. I've missed you so much." His mother pulled him into a big hug. Daniel grinned, really pleased to see her again, too, but he knew at once something was wrong.

"Where's Dad?" he asked, suddenly afraid of the answer.

"He's had to stay in America for a while, love. Let's go inside and I'll tell you all about it."

Later, after his mum had eaten and chatted to Aunt Jill and Amy for a short time, Daniel and his mum went for a walk together and she told him everything.

"I'm sorry, love, I know you'll be disappointed." She put her arm around his shoulder. "Your dad and I decided we need a little time apart, Daniel. He's going to stay with Uncle Ken for a wee bit longer and start his new job. Then we'll see how things go for a while. Maybe we can go over and visit him. He said to tell you he loves you, Daniel, and he'll miss you very much. He's going to phone you when we get home."

As he listened, Daniel was surprised not to feel more upset than he did. Of course, he'd miss his dad, but he wondered if Dad really would miss *him*. And he didn't want things to be exactly the same as before with his parents arguing all the time.

"It's okay, Mum, I understand. Maybe Dad just needs to see if it works out in America first." He needed to reassure her he could take it. She must be sad at coming home by herself.

"Oh, love, when did you get to be so wise? I think it's done you good being here."

Daniel smiled. Little did she know how scary it had been for a while. He thought about his mum and dad. Maybe if they had some time apart they would really miss each other and realise they had to be together. And maybe everything would be okay in the end. At least he wouldn't have to move away from Scotland at the moment.

"Jill said we can stay on here for another few days, Daniel. Would you like that?"

"Yeah, that'll be cool!" Daniel smiled at his mum and noticed the relief in her face. Maybe he'd feel differently about his dad being away when he had time to think about it, but right now he was just glad to see his mum back safely.

Later, Aunt Jill told him, "I have something for you, Daniel, to take home with you when it's time to leave."

Daniel stared at the thin rectangular shaped parcel. He hoped it wasn't the jigsaw. Maybe it was his painting.

"Go on, open it." Aunt Jill laughed. "It's not your own painting yet, I'm afraid. That has to dry before you can take it away. But I thought you might like one of mine."

So it was a painting. He started to pull the brown paper away. Somehow, he knew what it would be before he saw it. And there it was. The castle and knights dressed in armour.

"Wow, that's brilliant. Thanks, Aunt Jill. I love castles and things. Are you sure it's okay for me to have it?"

"It's meant for you. I thought you might like that kind of subject."

Daniel glanced at her strange, knowing smile again. He smiled back. It didn't mean anything. Most boys liked castles. And the dream was just a coincidence.

"That's been in the family a long time. I nearly forgot it was in a cupboard in the studio."

Daniel almost handed it back. So he hadn't seen it before? Then why did he suddenly start dreaming about castles? He looked over at Amy and his mum who were grinning at him. Too much imagination again. It was only a painting.

Later that evening Daniel and Amy took the jigsaw up to the attic and hid it beneath a pile of clothes in the old trunk.

"There, it can stay in the trunk forever," Amy said.

"Until someone else finds it one day," Daniel said. He closed the lid, glad to see it safely out of the way. Maybe they should have given it away or destroyed it, although he still thought the spell had disappeared for good.

As they climbed down the attic steps, Daniel paused for a moment. For just a second, he thought he'd heard the *tick, tock, tick, tock* of the old grandfather clock. Then he firmly closed the attic hatch door.

About the Author

Rosemary Gemmell is a prize-winning Scottish freelance writer of published short stories and articles in the UK, US, and online. She writes children's and teen stories as Ros and three of her children's stories were published in different anthologies, with stories for younger children published by Knowonder. She also writes adult historical and contemporary novels as Romy.

Rosemary is a member of her local writing group, the Scottish Association of Writers, the Romantic Novelists' Association, and the Society of Authors. She judges competitions and gives talks on writing and market research. She loves to share information on her blogs.

More information at: www.rosemarygemmell.com
and http://ros-readingandwriting.blogspot.com

Summer of the Eagles

Prologue

The boy stood still on one of the island's highest crags. From there he surveyed the wide terrain, right down to the slipway for the ferry coming over from the mainland. The latest influx of day trippers had arrived.

He saw the usual mixture of foot passengers, cyclists, and the cars that invaded his island. At one time, everyone walked or cycled into the island's small town.

The bus waited on the roadside at the top of the slipway for the foot passengers needing transport to Milltown five miles away. The boy's amber coloured eyes narrowed as he carefully studied each person. Two men caught his attention, their actions standing out from the rest. One was young and thin with a mean looking face. The other appeared heavier, older, and obviously annoyed for he already argued with the younger man.

As the boy watched, he knew those two were trouble. He understood people, with an unfailing instinct for their character. Even from this distance, he suspected they came for only one purpose. One that could mean danger for his kind. He'd need to keep a close watch on them.

Then his attention shifted to a girl and an old woman who stepped from the gangway. Something in the way the girl dragged along, almost behind the woman, suggested deep unhappiness. One leg seemed slightly shorter than the other, emphasised in the way she limped. The old woman looked kind but worried. She stopped now and then to speak to the girl, who only shrugged. Her behaviour peaked his interested despite himself. There seemed so much sadness between them. He wondered what caused it.

As the two arguing men walked towards the bus, he noticed the younger one turn and wave to the girl. She stared right through him before walking closer to the old woman.

Someone now met the females. Another woman - older than the girl, younger than the other. He thought about the drama now beginning, when these people stepped on to the island. It would unfold over these next weeks and he would be a part of it. He was ready.

A movement in the air above caught his eye and he smiled. Turning his back on the people below, he raised his arms and called out a greeting to the eagles swooping toward him.